Need a Trim, Jim

For the lady who gave me the idea - K.U.

For Joe Daniels
with love from MC

A Red Fox Book

Published by Random House Children's Books
20 Vauxhall Bridge Road, London SW1V 2SA

A division of The Random House Group Ltd
London Melbourne Sydney Auckland
Johannesburg and agencies throughout the world

Text copyright © Kaye Umansky 1999
Illustrations copyright © Margaret Chamberlain 1999

1 3 5 7 9 10 8 6 4 2

First published in Great Britain by The Bodley Head Children's Books 1999

Red Fox edition 2000

This book is sold subject to the condition that it shall not, by way of trade
or otherwise, be lent, resold, hired out, or otherwise circulated without the
publisher's prior consent in any form of binding or cover other than that in
which it is published and without a similar condition including this
condition being imposed on the subsequent purchaser.

The right of Kaye Umansky and Margaret Chamberlain to be identified as the
author and illustrator of this work has been asserted by them in accordance
with the Copyright, Designs and Patents Act, 1988.

Printed in Hong Kong by Midas Printing Ltd

THE RANDOM HOUSE GROUP Limited Reg. No. 954009
www.randomhouse.co.uk

ISBN 0 09 926546 X

Need A Trim, Jim

Kaye Umansky & Margaret Chamberlain

RED FOX

Look at Jim! He needs a trim.
His hair's so long, he cannot see.

He falls down stairs,

bumps into chairs

and has such trouble
with his tea.

He misses balls,

walks into walls

and you should see
him in the rain!

Come on, Jim, you need a trim.
It's time we saw your eyes again.

Hello, Clare! I *love* your hair!
You've had it cut, it's really cute.

There goes Pete, now, his is neat.
And goes so nicely with his suit.

Here comes Shirley, blonde and curly
(Twenty brush strokes every day!)
Gail has got a pony tail.
She says it keeps the flies away.

Dot has got an awful lot.
She wears it in a tidy plait.

Mike has spikes and Dave has waves
And George has gel to keep his flat.

What a lot of lovely hair styles
We've seen in the park today.

Looking forward to your trim, Jim?
What's that Jim? What did you say?

Does it hurt to have your hair cut?
Don't be silly. Not at all.

They simply take a pair of scissors...
Jim! Come back! Slow down, you'll fall!

Jim's escaping! Stop him, someone!
Ouch! He's run into a tree.

Now he's fallen in a puddle.

Now he's tripped and hurt his knee.

Poor old Jim. Cheer up. Don't cry.
You just can't see through all that hair.

Let's ask someone for a plaster.
There's a shop, just over there.

There, that's better. Feel more cheerful?
Got a tissue? Dry your face.

See the goldfish? Want a biscuit?
Isn't this a jolly place?

Let's make faces in the mirror.
Let's just pop you in the seat...

Snip, snip, snip! And there's your trim, Jim!
Honest, Jim. You look real sweet.